nick jr.

nick jr.
Nella
THE PRINCESS KNIGHT

THE SHARE FAIR

adapted from the teleplay "The Share Faire"
by Liam Farrell

by Delphine Finnegan

illustrated by Nneka Myers

Random House New York

There was a craft fair at Princess Nella's school one day.

Everyone made crafts
to share.

Princess Nella and Trinket made tiaras. They used beautiful flowers.

The two friends
could not wait
to share their tiaras!

Sir Garrett and Clod
made funny
sock puppets.

Willow and Minatori made yummy lemonade.

Everyone wanted
Nella and Trinket's tiaras!

Sir Blaine was not happy.
No one wanted
his balloon swords.

Sir Blaine snuck behind
Nella and Trinket's stand.
He knocked dirt
all over their flowers.

Oh, no!
The dirt flattened
the flowers.

Nella cleaned off
the flowers.
She had an idea.

She made necklaces
with the flat flowers.
Everybody wanted one!

Sir Blaine had
a new plan.
He stretched a balloon
to fling the flowers away!

Nella and Trinket caught the flowers!

But all the petals fell off.

Nella made bracelets
from the stems!

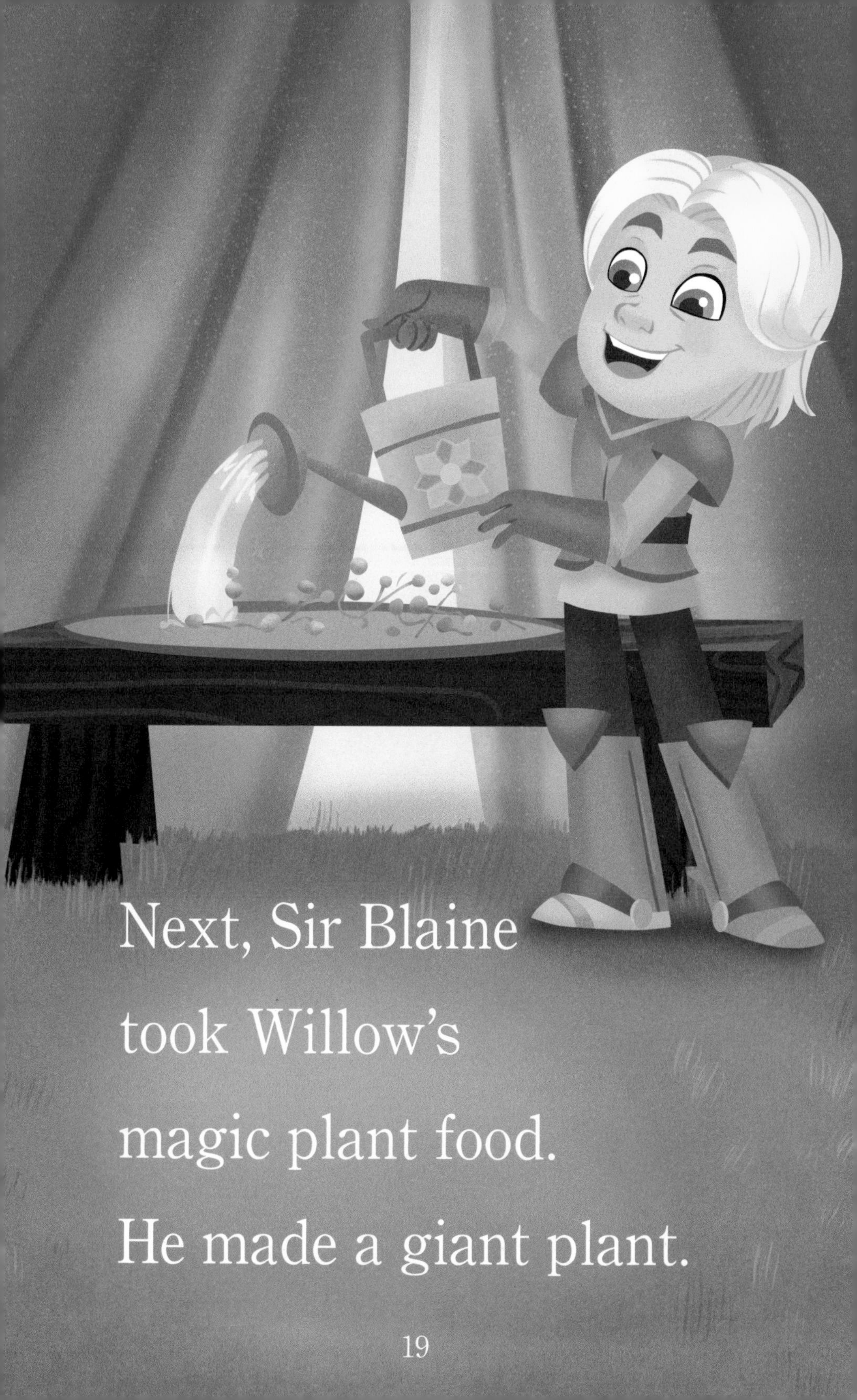

Next, Sir Blaine
took Willow's
magic plant food.
He made a giant plant.

The giant plant
grabbed Sir Blaine!

Nella knew what to do.
She turned into
a Princess Knight!

Nella used Sir Blaine's balloons to rescue him.

The fair was saved.

Everyone cheered!

Sir Blaine thanked Nella
with a balloon tiara
and sword.